Poop on the Shoe
A Potty Training Whodunit!

Written by
Jeremy Blankenship

Illustrated by
Kim K Whittemore

Dedicated
to all the
future Rulers
of the "Throne"

To Eva and Mila,
may you always know
where to go.
   -Jeremy

For everyone
who truly understands
that it's all about
the poop.
   -Kim

I don't know!
Where do FISH poop?

Was it a FISH?

In the pasture!

In the forest!

ON THE POTTY!

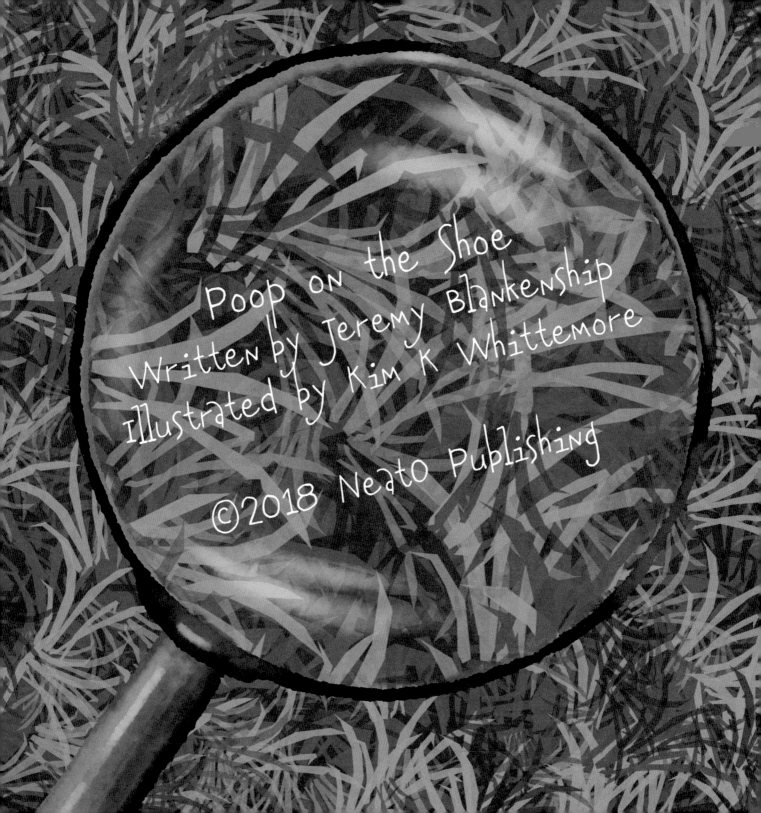

Poop on the Shoe
Written by Jeremy Blankenship
Illustrated by Kim K Whittemore